How To Make Anyone Fall In Love With You Within Minutes

Marianne Kolb

C/O IMPRESSUM-SERVICE
VALLEETSY
PADRE BURGOS AVE,
1000 METRO MANILA

Table Of Contents

Foreword

How to Make Anyone Fall in Love with You Within Minutes is a special labor of love from us. When most people saw this title for the first time, they thought I was talking out of my hat! I met people who were completely sure that you could not make anyone fall in love with you in a whole lifetime if they were not interested. But, then, aren't there people who believe in love at first sight as well, and scores of people who never think twice before professing their loves to anybody? So, the ocean is wide on both sides. Which side should we go then?

Our ultimate intention here is to make people fall in love with you, and that too in such a way that they become a constructive force in your life. Love is something that can give you strength if you find it from the right person. Here, you are going to see a hitherto unspoken aspect of love... the fact that you can make anyone fall in love with you as soon as you want them to.

Of course, there are things to do. You have to put in efforts. Maybe you will have to make some adjustments within yourself too. But, if your current demeanor isn't giving you the things you want, wouldn't it be advisable to make those alterations? After all, at the end of the rope, you have a totally different 'you'... a person whom people cannot wait to fall in love with.

How To Make Anyone Fall In Love With You Within Minutes Uncover The Hidden Chemistry And Find Your True Love

Chapter 1:
Analyzing Yourself

Synopsis

When you are trying to make someone love you, the one most important thing you need is to be fully acquainted with yourself. Keep this in mind... people are going to fall in love with you only if you have a personality that impresses them; only if they know that they will get what they want from you.

But, if you have to assure people of that, it is necessary that you build for yourself such a personality. So, how do you make those improvements? You begin by understanding completely where you stand at the moment.

Be completely sure of what you are... what you are capable of. Understand what it is that people are looking for. Understand what's lacking in you. What are the positive points you can play on? What are the negative traits you should try to eliminate? If you want to continue having a magnetic personality that attracts people, you should begin by analyzing yourself and making those corrections when needed.

What Is Love?

Our theme here is love. Whatever we are going to talk about in the following pages, it is going to lead to the same conclusion... *how to make people fall in love with us, within minutes.*

Is that possible? Certainly it is. People can fall in love with you the very instant they set their eyes in you. But, that doesn't mean you shouldn't work towards it. It is not going to happen automatically. You have to put in effort. And this effort begins much before that first sight which can kindle love.

So, what is love? I would say, *love is acceptance.*

If you love someone, it means you accept them as they are, with their faults and weaknesses. You make their joys and sorrows their own. You are happy in their happiness; you are distressed when they are distressed. And it works the other way round too.

When someone falls in love with you, it means they should accept you the way you are. They should not try to change anything about you, because that is very unlikely to happen.

The first thing you need to get started is to know what love is. It is only when you understand the true meaning of love will you acknowledge it when someone falls in love with you.

Love needn't be worn on the sleeve all the time. Maybe someone is loving you right now and you don't know it. Look around you. Think about the people you know. Is there someone who is quite happy with what you are, loves your company, makes plans with you and wants to

be with you? Perhaps that's the person for you. Perhaps not. But, give it a thought. There are too many people you have around you, even if you are a complete introvert. Sit down and analyze... have you found your love already and don't know it?

If you don't have the correct perspective of love, then you will not understand it when it comes your way. You will have wasted an opportunity. And that's not the point of this book.

It is not always like they show in the movies. When you fall in love, you won't hear bells chiming or guitars playing. In fact, most people realize only later that they are in love with a particular person.

Remember the main point that love is acceptance. If you are ready to accept someone as they are, and if they are ready to accept you as you are, then you have scored already.

Your Strengths and Your Weaknesses

A lot of people are selfish to the point to impudence. They expect the best in their partners but they do not take a look at themselves. They are too busy dealing with how their perfect man or woman should be, but they do not bother about their own selves. That is why most times we end up expecting too much than what we deserve. Now, it is not that we should not build high expectations, but dreaming in vain serves no purpose. It only leads to heartbreak when things do not go the way we want. And, if you cannot cut your coat according to your cloth, such heartbreak is more likely to happen.

So, you need to begin with a little introspection first. Start by finding out what you are good at… and what you are not good at. Think from the other person's point of view. How do they consider you? What, do they think, are your strengths and weaknesses?

Make a list of all those points. Write them down. When you see words taking shape in front of you, they make a better impact on the mind.

Be honest with yourself. This list is only for you, no one else is going to see it, so you can be as frank with it as you want. It does not matter if your weaknesses are far too many in comparison to your strengths.

Once you have this list ready, start planning your strategies. You have to think of a two-pronged approach.

→ You have to think what you can do to correct your weaknesses, and
→ You have to think what you can do to enhance your strengths.

Everyone has imperfections, but not everyone realizes them. The very fact that you can come out of denial and accept the shortcomings within you will mean a lot to you. Acceptance is always the first step of improvement.

Some of these weaknesses will be trivial things… things like you do not know how to dance, you do not know how to approach people, you have a habit of not listening to people when they are conversing with you, and so on. It is easy to improve upon them. Some of them may be severe, such as financial problem or a health problem. See what you can do to improve upon it.

At the same time, do not forget the underlying theme here... a person truly loves you only if they can accept you as they are.

But that does not mean you do not try and improve yourself whenever you can. If you want someone to fall in love with you, then it is your responsibility to be a better person for them as well.

Also, do not ignore your strengths. If you have something that could be great in a relationship, work on them a little more. See how you can improve there. A little education never hurts. Practice your expertise to perfection. Often, people will ignore your weaknesses if your strengths are too great.

So, that is where you start... understanding what love is, and then understanding what kind of a person you are. When you have these two things firmly entrenched in your mind, you are on your way to finding love at the drop of a hat!

Chapter 2:
Changing the Way You Think

Synopsis

If you want to develop a wonderful personality that always impresses people, then you have to begin with self-improvement. We already talked about self-realization in the previous chapter, where you analyze yourself truthfully and see where you stand. Now, when you are better aware of what kind of person you are, the next step would be to improve upon yourself.

When we are talking about love—whether it is about falling in it or making others fall in love with you—the most important thing is to improve the mind. You have to have a clear thought process. You should not let your mind be riddled with negativism and pessimism. You have to keep the hope alive.

A positive mindset is what everyone likes. You cannot expect anyone to fall in love with you when you are a brooding, depressed or angry personality.

We shall talk here about the mindset you should project if you want to make people fall in love with you. If you want, this mindset can be created within a day. If you don't, it will take ages but you won't be able to change the way you think.

What Do You Think about Yourself?

More than the impact of any other influence on your mind is the impact of your own thinking. What do you think about yourself? You will find that most people become what they think about themselves.

I am a teacher. I teach kids at a very impressionable age... they are between 14 and 16 years when I teach them. I recall an incident with a boy I was teaching. His name was Mark Munay. Mark was an exceptionally brilliant kid, especially talented in Math. He could work problems that children two years his senior could not.

And then one day, one of his school teachers happened to tell him that Mark should not attempt a particular chapter—it was Matrices— because it was beyond his level.

I knew that Mark knew how to solve matrices because he had solved some of those problems for me the week before.

But the school teacher's influence was greater. A negative influence is always more impactful. Since the teacher told him that the chapter was beyond his level, and since he told it in a very emphatic manner, Mark settled that in his head. After that, he never worked Matrices well, not even two years later when he was of the age when children normally learn the topic.

This happened because Mark told himself he could not do it. He let an external influence decide what he was capable of.

Knowingly or unknowingly, we let that happen to ourselves too. Whether these people mean well or not, they often disorient us. Our

family, our friends, our employers, our teachers... they all tell us things that we use to build an impression about ourselves.

If only we could sit and allow our minds to decide what we are capable of! Things would be so different then!

If you are thinking why people all around you are finding love and why you are behind in the race, then probably you need to look within your own mind first. Have you built some invisible barricades around yourself? Probably you are telling yourself that you are not worthy of love. Probably you are stopping yourself from reaching out to people on account of that. It is because of such things that people start looking at you negatively too.

After all, if you look at yourself myopically, people are going to do the same.

There are two things you have to bear in mind here...

→ Never think that you are incapable of anything. Doesn't matter how difficult or unattainable that objective seems at the moment; don't let it limit your potential.

→ Think beyond what you can achieve. Always. Always keep challenging yourself. Whether you are chasing your personal growth or professional growth or looking for a relationship, always try further than people tell you can go. If you have belief in yourself, that should be more than enough to keep you going.

How Optimistic Can You Be?

Following from our previous discussion, we come to a very important point here.

You have to be _optimistic_.

If you give it a thought, it is optimism that has kept us going all through the ages. If it weren't for hope, people would have given up, communities would have faltered, countries would have perished, the world wouldn't have sustained itself the way it has. Optimism has kept us alive all through.

And, now, when you are hoping that people will fall in love with you, it will be optimism that will illuminate your path.

What is optimism? In the Oxford Dictionary, it is defined as:-

Optimism (n): hopefulness and confidence about the future or the success of something

In our context, when you are optimistic, you are hopeful that people will love you. That is, they will appreciate you and accept you for what you are.

Do you think that will happen? Are you apprehensive about acceptance? If you harbor such apprehensions within yourself, then these apprehensions manifest themselves outwardly as well. If you don't have confidence within, people can sense it. They can understand that you are not on a sure footing. This can jeopardize your chances of finding love, and finding success in anything.

If your intention is to succeed... in anything... then the most important thing is to build an unflagging amount of confidence within yourself. This comes through optimism. Be hopeful that positive things will happen. That will give you the confidence to try out new things. That will give you the confidence to approach people in the way you should.

In improving your way of thinking, a very important contribution is of how positively you can think. Shun all the debilitating thoughts and move ahead.

Believe in the Law of Attraction, which says...

Like attracts like.

If you think positive, then positive things are going to happen to you. If you believe staunchly that something will happen, then everything around you will align itself in such a way that these things start taking shape. That's the power of optimism. Be optimistic, and you will find things actually happening the way you believe them to be.

Chapter 3:
Your Interactions with People

Synopsis

Finding love is a highly social activity. You are not going to do it by being with yourself. You have to go out and deal with people.

And, not only do you have to deal with people, but you have to deal with them in such a manner that they bring positive results.

Hence, your interactions with people mean a lot. If you want to make others fall in love with you, this is something you have to work on.

Here we are going to deal with three main aspects:-

→ How to reach out to people so that you may find the one you want to fall in love with,

→ How to interact with them, and

→ How to create a lasting impression on them so that they do not forget you, but want to meet you again.

Reaching Out—Being an Extrovert

One of the most important things for you in your mission of finding love is to reach out to people. People are all around you, and the one you want to fall in love with you is also out there. These people will not come walking to you. You have to take yourself to them. Or, at least, you have to be visible to them.

Hence, being an introvert definitely does not help. You have to be an extrovert... you have to take yourself out into the open.

Now, being an extrovert is quite a subjective thing. The concept is different from one person to another. For some people, being an extrovert means that they have to go out and participate in sports and do some adventurous things and roam all over the world. For some others, simply going to church means being an extrovert. You may have your own definition... but what I am telling you here is that you have to mingle with people.

Widen your social circle. Get in touch with as many people as you can. And, since you are trying to find a relationship here, it will really work if you move about in places that suit your interests, because those are the places in which you will find people that meet your requirements.

So, join a club. Start going to church regularly. Go out and meet friends. Do not turn down those party invitations. Join a good online dating website. Help people do things. Move out in society. Talk to people. Discuss and share problems and experiences. These are all different ways in which you become visible. These are ways in which people begin to notice you. They start knowing you exist. You don't need to sell yourself; just be what you are, but only be more social.

Basic Things to Remember When Interacting in Society

When you interact with people, you should realize that you are creating impressions on them all the time. People are constantly monitoring you, knowingly or unknowingly. You do not understand how and when that happens, but it does. You say something, and that is the thing on which they will judge you. The way you dress will decide what kind of impression they have on you. Why, even if you simply wear your hair in a particular way, people are going to start talking about it!

You can definitely not please anyone, and you shouldn't try you. That is not the way you can gain love. And even if you meet up with somebody by being who you really aren't, it won't last long. Better alone than such a relationship!

However, some things you can do can help build better impressions on people. These are all constructive things; things that you would do well to keep in mind.

→ Know when to talk and when to listen. Sometimes, the person with you will want to say something. At other times, they will not want to talk much. You have to take the cue from their mannerisms and behavior. This is being respectful to their mood, a very important quality to develop.

→ Always be a better listener. When you hear out what people are saying, you are expressing your concern. People always love a listener. At the same time, do not be a mute listener. Show that you are paying attention. Intersperse the conversation with well-placed interjections. Ask relevant questions to let the other person say.

→ When speaking, do not go on and on about yourself. Say something that doesn't sound like you are boasting. In fact, you have to just inform people about yourself... never delve too much on it. But, don't be a clam either. People do not like to have relationships with clams.

→ Get to know the other person. This is extremely important. Remember their name, understand what they do, find out about their family if it seems appropriate, etc. And remember these things the next time they meet. Address them by name. You will probably cinch the deal there and then.

→ Show concern to the other people around you. For example, if you are seated at a restaurant, then do not disrespect the garcon! The way you deal with people is often a factor for judging you. While some people take pride in demeaning other people, the people with them get a very low opinion of them.

→ Never invite people too bluntly. Invitations should seem like they are deserved. You should never invite people just for the heck of it because then it seems inappropriate and even insulting. And, don't create events just so you can invite people. Those tricks are old; they do not work anymore.

→ Smile a lot. Do not miss any opportunity to smile. A grumpy face never does anyone any good.

→ Be knowledgeable. Read the papers. Browse the Internet. Find out what is happening in the world around you. When you enhance your knowledge, you have things to talk. And, when you have things to talk, people enjoy your company.

→ Do not push too hard. This is a very important point to remember. When you are trying to strike an acquaintance, you should not come across as desperate. You should maintain your dignity. You should know when to back off. You will find the person who deserves you very soon.

Creating an Impression on People

I have one thing to say about creating impressions on people. You should never come across as shallow. Just be your true self, and you will find that that always works.

Of course, an important part of our agenda here is to be able to create the right impression on people. We are going to try that too, but pushing the envelope too much doesn't work either.

The way I always advocate this is as follows...

First, improve your personality. Be a better person from within. Then, try to meet people in the manner that's the most natural to you. This is the best way to impress people.

You need to take your natural personality take over. If needed, enhance your personality. But do not put on a personality on an ad-hoc basis. You can develop your personality, but you should never role-play for just one particular situation.

So, be a good conversationalist, do not have too many secrets, be concerned for other people around you, be expressive, dress neatly, speak well... these are the things that help creating the first favorable impression. We just spoke about it in the previous part of this chapter, so we are not going to go down that alley again.

But the one message that I want to reiterate is that you need to be your natural self. Develop your personality as a consistent effort, and then approach people in the most casual, genuine manner. This is what is sure to impress everyone you meet.

Chapter 4:
Improving Yourself Physically

Synopsis

To a very high extent, love is influenced by your physicality. Nature has devised us in such a manner that we are impressed by a person's looks. The initial spark of love is often dictated by how a person looks. However, you should not get the wrong meaning here.

Though your good looks are good enough as a starting point, they are not enough to sustain you in the long run. Eventually, it is the person you are that matters; your looks can only take you so far.

However, as a starting point, it is good to focus on your looks. You should not completely underestimate the importance of your physical self in attracting your paramour. That is going to happen. So, pay attention to your looks. Be vain, to a point!

Why Is Your Body Important?

There are a lot of connotations to love. One of them is the purely physical one. After all, the basic meaning of love is still the physical act. And, this is triggered by the attraction... attraction towards how a person looks. We are all attracted by good-looking people, and that is where the very first flame starts to flicker. Most times, this kind of attraction is just infatuation, and that should not be mistaken as love. But, even when we are talking of the pure and sublime true love, physical appeal does work!

Scientists have unearthed various mysteries of the mechanism of love (though a lot of them still remain what they are—mysteries!) and among these mysteries we know of pheromones. All of us exude some hormones in the environment called as pheromones. These have no scent or any other mark, but they are inexplicably understood by people of the opposite sex.

And it triggers some kind of response in them. This is why man is attracted to woman and vice-versa.
It is the pheromones at work. And that is a purely physical thing.

Now, though there is no relation between pheromones and a person's visual attractiveness, that does seem to be the case. Otherwise, why else will some people be more of a opposite gender magnet and some would repel? At the same time, this is confusing. There are people who look quite plain but are always found with people of the opposite sex. And attractive people are sometimes found alone!

We do not know yet what this mechanism of physical attraction is, or how it works, but it seems best to play along with the majority. And
the majority feels that they are physically attracted towards good- looking people.

It should not hurt you to improve the way you look. This is not objectification; it is the way nature has ordained us to be. After all, when we like to look at good-looking people, shouldn't the equation work the other way round as well?

A part of your physical self includes being healthy. You are sure to accept this... if you are healthy, you are more attractive to people. If you are fit and fine, people will want to be with you all the more. Why would anyone be sadistic enough to be with a sickly person anyway?

So, to sum it up, these are the things you should really focus on:-

→ Keep your weight in check.

→ Keep fit with regular exercise.

→ Do not become a cosmetic king or queen but do take care of the way you look.

→ Get a smart haircut.

→ Embellish yourself in any way you want.

→ Improve upon any health defects you may have.

Pay attention to these things closely. You may not be able to achieve all of these in a day, but do keep them up as a consistent process. Even when someone falls in love with you, you cannot stop doing these things. You owe it to your partner to keep looking good!

Tips to Improve Your Body

Now, you are probably not intending to become the most handsome or beautiful person in the world, but there are a few things you can do to improve your physical being.

→ Think about your body first. You have to get your body in shape. The best way to go about it is exercise. Go for a jog or at least a brisk walk every morning. This will help you stay fitter and, more importantly, it will give you a clear time to think each morning. The solitary thinking time you get every morning is a veritable perk.

→ Eat moderately. Avoid the high carbs and the high calories. Do not gorge on fatty food, however much tempted you might feel. Instead, chomp on those veggies and fresh foods. Instead of red meats, consume more of lean meats. Drink about 8 to 10 glasses of water every day.

Never fill your stomach to its full capacity.

→   Give your body the pampering treatment occasionally. Go for a nice haircut, and do not underestimate the power of those manicures and pedicures as well. Keep your salon appointments going on; they help you feel good about yourself.

→ Just before you are starting out with exercise, have a cup of coffee. The caffeine present in it will stimulate you to do more exercise. Also, this combination has been recommended by specialists for optimizing the body's workouts.

→ Listen to music when you are exercising. This makes exercising more pleasurable. You must choose your music wisely. If you choose something that has quick, peppy beats, then your body is going to work out in the same rhythm as well.

→ Have a lot of salads. One thing that you should definitely add in your salad is avocado. This enhances the effect of vitamin A in the salad. Vitamin A is abundant in foods such as carrots.

→ If you eat something that is high in fat, eat a little yogurt afterward. Yogurt has significant calcium content. The calcium will adhere to the fatty acids and prevent them from getting absorbed in the body.

→ Choose your foods wisely. Choose everything that is organic. Stay away from foods that are laden with preservatives and other synthetic chemicals. These are going to harm your body in various ways in the long run and slow down the metabolism.

→ Feed your mind with positive thoughts and enriching knowledge. When your mind is enhanced, your body is improved as well. Spend some time in meditation each day. This will give you clarity of thought and you will be able to plan things in a more concise manner.

→ Work hard, and then rest hard! Your body needs to find the sense of gratification. It cannot feel contented unless you use it to do constructive work. Then, you must make sure that you get adequate rest. Do this on a daily basis. When you work to your maximum capacity and then rest deservedly, your body gets a

particular kind of glow... it sends out a great aura that adds to its appeal.

Do these things consistently. Pay attention to your body and you will see that its attractiveness begins to increase. This is highly important.

When your body becomes attractive, you are automatically 'in the eyes of people'. People cannot resist looking at you. Your goals of finding someone who finds you attractive are met!

Chapter 5:
Improving Your Personality

Synopsis

Your personality is what you are. It is your characteristic, your identity. You are nothing without it. But, at the same time, you have to ensure that you have a personality that people find impressive. Since you are trying to find love here, which becomes very important. You need people to find your personality warm and welcoming and attractive. How can you do that?

What Is Personality?

To put it quite simply, personality is the sum total of your mental buildup and the way you behave. It is made up of the way you express yourself, the way you react to things, the way you perform your tasks and even the opinions that you have about things that happen around you. All these make up your personality.

Personality becomes a very important aspect of any individual. It is your personality that eventually tells people who you are. As humans, we are prone to create impressions in our mind about the people that we meet. Your personality is a very important factor in the kind of impression you generate for people around you. It is possible that even before you meet someone, they have heard about you and they have some kind of an idea what you are like. This happens because personality creates impressions... it actually stereotypes you.

You may feel this is wrong. After all, why should people think in advance about how you are going to behave? But that is the way we are. That is the way you are as well. Before meeting someone of the opposite gender, there is a likelihood that people will tell you about them. You then develop an impression about them. So, when you approach someone, you are almost never totally blank. You already have an idea of what kind of people they are.

That brings us to a very important aspect of our ultimate goal... how to make anyone fall in love with you within minutes.

And that aspect is... you have to work on your personality.

If you have a personality that is considered to be attractive, a personality that people are bound to appreciate, then you can rest easy. It is this kind of personality that will attract other people. They will want to hobnob with you. They will want to be seen with you. This is what creates the initial attraction.

It is your personality that brings people to you and keeps them drawn to you initially. After that, it depends on how you take it further. However, if you want the initial interest to be created, you have to make sure that you have a personality that can enamor people.

That will include not just your physique, but also the way you think, the way you dress and perhaps even the way you hold your fork and spoon when you are eating. Unknown to you, people are judging you whenever you are visible. One of the most important things in your agenda is to have a personality that people are willing to accept.

How to Develop a Personality that Dazzles Everyone

So, what can you do to build that personality that everyone just seems to fall in love with? Is this an easy process?

Building your personality to be at its impressive best is certainly not an easy job. A personality isn't something that you can just switch on or off. But at the same time, remember that personality can be changed.

The word personality comes from the Latin word **'persona'** *which means* **'mask'***.*

That gives you a very important clue. If personality is meant to be a mask, it means you can wear it. You can hone your personality to be exactly what you want it to be.

If you want your personality to be more attractive to people, there are ways and means of achieving it.

Read on to know some ways in which you can create a dazzling personality that impresses anyone you meet.

Be Confident

Confidence is the first and most important trait of your personality. When faced with any situation, you need to be confident about it. You need to know what it is about and you need to have a confident way of handling it. It is only this kind of approach that people like. When you are confident, you are impressing people because you are projected as a credible person, a person who will soon meet with success.

Be Knowledgeable

It is necessary to know how to do important things. There are things you should know, like how to drive a car, how to swim, how to speak French... whatever fits your context. People are impressed by such things. But, it is not just these practical things that you have to be knowledgeable about. You have to be worldly-wise. You have to know how things work in society. When someone is with you and facing a problem, you should be able to give them a knowledgeable opinion. This is one of the most important things if you are looking at impressing people.

Be Informed

Read your papers. Watch the news. Check the Internet for current happenings. Always be aware of what is happening in the world around you. This helps you open up conversations and sustain them. Also, everyone is impressed by well-informed people. So, try to be updated on current affairs at all times.

Dress Well

Now, that does not mean you should get the most expensive clothes that you see, but you have to dress gracefully. Keep up with current fashion trends and dress to the occasion. People always like to see smartly-dressed people.

Get Good at Conversation

We have already spoken about this in a previous chapter so we can skim through this point. However, you need to ensure that you are a great conversationalist. Listen more than you speak, and speak relevant and meaningful things that can take the conversation forward. Also, make sure that you give the other person their due importance when you are speaking with them.

These are the basic things that you have to pay attention to. There are many other things that you can inculcate as you keep growing. Remember to evolve your personality at all times—this is the most important factor people are going to see you by.

Chapter 6:
The Approach

Synopsis

Getting someone to fall in love with you might seem to be an uphill task, but everything depends on the initial approach. How you meet people is important. In fact, how a person responds to you depends largely on the way that you approach them. Here we shall take a look at the methods of approach that work, and what you can do to improve your approach towards people.

How to Approach Someone
You Want to Fall in Love with You

Everything that we have spoken about in this book so far has been towards this end... approaching someone with the intention that they should fall in love with you. This is what I have given you tips on so far. Tips on how you can create a dazzling personality and the right demeanor so that when you approach someone for the first time, you meet with the words you want to hear.

So, you see someone you find interesting. They look great and you would really want to hang out with them. But, do you want them to fall in love with you? Or the other way round? Maybe not yet. It is advisable to first find out about the other person and see whether you really want to hook up with them. Remember that it is love we are talking about here, not infatuation.

Once you have thoroughly decided that you want this person to fall in love with you, you can make your move.

How do you approach them? Here are some tips.

→ The first thing you would need is confidence. Do not be shaky or jittery; that would only show you in a bad light. You are a person, they are a person as well. Maybe they have similar thoughts in their mind too. Keep this in mind. Do not be cowed down by the fear of failure. Keep your spirits high and sally on.

→ Do not be worried of the result. Do not think too far into the future. Maybe just a casual date is good for the moment. Do not expect more than that. That way, whatever happens, you will not be affected too much.

→ Be casual. Do not put on an act. Most importantly, do not rehearse. Just think for a moment what you will say and then go on. If you think too much, things may belie your expectations.

→ Be sincere when you approach them. Look at them in the eye, but do not leer. Have a smile on your face. Look cool but not imposing. Do not put on a face that shows you are bored of all these things! At the same time, do not appear overeager like a schoolboy. Be your normal self.

→ Do not let a previous rejection faze you. If you have tried the approach with someone else before and it has not worked, there is no reason why it should not work this time as well. Every person is different. It is not necessary to change your approach. What did not work for someone may work this time.

These are some things that you have to keep in mind. Most importantly, do not hesitate. Make the move. Whatever happens, you should not let the result affect you too much.

The First Date

So, you won the chance for a first date with someone. Felicitations! Now, what do you do? What do you do to ensure this date goes well and things hit off between the two of you?

Here are some tips.

1. Choose a location where both of you would be comfortable. Most people try to impress their first date partners by selecting the most important place on the list. This is not necessary. If you go to a five star restaurant and are more worried about the right way to sit, what fun is there on your first date? Instead, go to a place where you can both be at ease and can just look forward to spending time with each other.

2. At the same time, a little bit of entertainment on your first date can be a good idea, especially if you do not know the other person at all. These things could be icebreakers. You could go for a bowling date or even a movie date. Discussing the movie at the end of it can be a great conversation starter between the two of you.

3. Do not overdress. It is a very bad impression... you should not look overeager. Be your own casual self, but at the same time, do take the pains to select an elegant everyday dress. Also, if you are used to dressing sexily even on your normal days, avoid that on your first date. Do not dress provocatively. That might send the impression that you are only looking for a sexual encounter. Dress what suits you best and what you are most comfortable in.

4. Have great conversation throughout your first date. Let there not be a moment of silence… avoid those awkward pauses. At the same time, there are some things you need to avoid talking about on your first date. Do not talk about the problems in your life. You don't want to saddle a strange person with your job travails. Do not speak about things that they may have a strong

opinion about, like the tax system in your state. Speak on neutral topics, topics that you are sure will be good for conversation and not too polarizing.

5. Most importantly, do not expect too much from the other person on your first date. Do not judge them all the time. They are just as nervous as you are. If you are slipping up, chances are that they are slipping up too. In fact, you should do your best to make them feel at ease. Avoid those prying looks into their plate to see what they are eating, for example.

6. Pay attention to the date. Do not get distracted. Do not think too much about what food to order, what movie to watch, etc. Your attention should be focused on spending time with the person you are with.

7. When parting, be casual. Do not tell them that you will call them if you won't. Do not force a second date. Both of you need some time and space to think whether you want to do it again; it is in your best interests. Should you kiss on your first date? That definitely depends on how the date went. Was there any chemistry between the two of you?

Keep these things in mind when you are on your first date. You want your first date to be a success if you want the other person to fall in love with you.

Chapter 7:
Getting What You Want

Synopsis

So, have you got everything you need to fulfill your desire? Here is a checklist of them.

Checklist of All the Things You Need

To wind it all up, here are the things that you should need if you want to make people fall in love with you in minutes:-

Know About Yourself

The first person you need to get to know better is yourself. What is it within you that you can tone down or improve? Can you pinpoint where you need to make these adjustments? What aspects of you are already cool, and you can make them better? Analyze your personality. Try bettering what you have.

Improve Your Mindset

It is very important to have the right thought process. Be clear in the way you think, and be optimistic. Never let your thoughts or other people's impression about you bog you down. Keep up the confidence and move on progressively.

Improve Your Equation with People

You also need to improve your relationships in society. Come out of that shell. Do not be introverted; come out and interact with people. It is only when you meet people will you find someone you like. Also, if you want people to be interested in you, it is important to be visible to them.

Work Out Your Body

Contrary to what anyone says, your physical appearance matters. Improve your physique. You have to look appealing and attractive, if not the most handsome or beautiful person in the world.

Develop Your Personality

You have to be a suave, confident person if you want to impress people with your personality. You have to have the right knowledge about things. You have to be a well-informed person and good at conversation. These are the things that matter.

Work on all these aspects. When you have these vital ingredients ready, your first impressions become more profound. You become better geared at making people fall in love with you!

Wrapping Up

Now you have it all... the basic ingredients you need to initiate your love life and take it in the right direction. Work on them. You won't be able to do it instantly, probably, but consistent effort will make you the love magnet you hope to be.

It is all about making the start. So, proceed, and all the best!